W9-BFP-823

BONNIE PRYOR

Birthday Blizzard

ILLUSTRATED BY
MOLLY DELANEY

MORROW JUNIOR BOOKS • NEW YORK

To Jeanne, a country friend
with a winter birthday
—B. P.

To Jane
—M. D.

Printed in Hong Kong by South China Printing Company (1988) Ltd.

1 2 3 4 5 6 7 8 9 10

Library of Congress Cataloging-in-Publication Data
Pryor, Bonnie.
Birthday blizzard / Bonnie Pryor ; illustrated by Molly Delaney. p. cm.
Summary: Jamie is disappointed when a huge blizzard cancels her birthday party, until unexpected visitors arrive to create a winter picnic and a very special birthday.
ISBN 0-688-09423-6.—ISBN 0-688-09424-4 (lib. bdg.)
[1. Blizzards—Fiction. 2. Snow—Fiction. 3. Birthdays—Fiction. 4. Parties—Fiction.]
I. Delaney, Molly, ill. II. Title. PZ7.P94965Bi 1993 [E]—dc20 92-1713 CIP AC

The night before Jamie's birthday a blizzard roared through town.

"My party!" she cried, waking up late at night. Outside, the wind blustered and bellowed. Inside, the house creaked and snapped. It was *cold*.

Usually Jamie loved snow, but not now. She thought about the hats and favors and prizes for games that were stacked in bright piles on the kitchen table. She wiggled her feet into her new Christmas slippers and raced to her parents' bedroom. Her father was already stirring.

"There's a terrible storm," Jamie cried. "Can't you hear it? And my party is tomorrow."

"It's just a train," said her mother's sleepy voice. Then she sat straight up. "There are no trains around here."

The three of them huddled by the window, staring as the wild wind pushed mountains of snow against the house.

"This looks much worse than predicted," said Daddy. "Come back to bed. Maybe by morning it will have stopped."

The words hung hopefully around the room, and Jamie slept wrapped in her parents' warmth.

But at daybreak the wind still howled and the snow clung to the windows.

"I'll never make it to work today," Daddy said.

"Will I still have my party?" Jamie was trying not to cry.

"I'm afraid no one will get here in this weather," Mama said. "But later we can have a cozy party just for three."

Jamie couldn't believe it. "It's not fair!" she wailed. "Why wasn't I born in the summertime?"

"Jamie, *please*," said her father. Then he smiled. "Think of it as an adventure. How many people get to have blizzards on their birthdays?"

"It doesn't feel like an adventure," Jamie said. "It just feels cold."

"The electricity is out. That means no furnace. And no T.V.," Daddy added, when Jamie tried to switch it on.

Mama moved the party decorations off the kitchen table. She wrapped Jamie up in a woolly blanket, and Daddy piled wood in the living-room fireplace. In a corner of the basement he found the camp stove and portable heater packed away with the tent.

Mama put new batteries in the radio. They listened to the news while she made cocoa on the stove. Jamie rolled herself into a grumbly ball.

Good
milk!

"Hundreds of travelers are stranded on the roads," said the announcer. "It's the worst storm in twenty years."

"I wonder if Mr. and Mrs. Piper are all right," said Mama. "They don't have a working fireplace to keep them warm. I tried to call, but the phone's dead too."

Jamie groaned. The Pipers were very old. Mrs. Piper talked too loud and pinched her cheek, and Mr. Piper hardly talked at all.

The Pipers had two sturdy work horses. They were too old to pull a wagon or a plow anymore, but Jamie liked to stroke their soft, velvety noses and watch them clomp across the field next door.

"What about Gabe and Donney?" she asked, suddenly worried. She could just see the roof of the big red barn from their living-room window.

"Let's go find out," Daddy said. Mama helped Jamie get ready. She put plastic bags over Jamie's socks before helping her on with her boots.

"That looks silly," Jamie grumbled.

"It will keep your feet warm," Daddy told her. He wrapped a scarf around her nose.

"We look like bank robbers." Jamie giggled.

"Fat bank robbers," Daddy said.

The snow had stopped falling at last, but it was so deep, Jamie could hardly walk. The icy wind hurt to breathe. "Do you want to go back?" asked Daddy.

Jamie thought about Gabe and Donney and shook her head.

"Walk in my footprints," Daddy said.

Snow covered the pasture, but Jamie kept her eyes on the Pipers' old farmhouse and bravely followed. Sometimes her father had to give her a tug. When they stopped at the barn, he had to throw his whole weight against the sliding door to get it open.

The horses were inside, looking warm enough in their shaggy winter coats. They stomped their feet, and steam puffed out when they snorted hello. Daddy gave them hay and some fresh water. “That should hold them for a while,” he said.

"Look at those tracks," Jamie said when they were back out in the snow.

"They look like a small dog's," Daddy decided. "Poor thing. I hope it found someplace safe from the storm." Together they struggled across the yard, trying to stamp down the snow as they went.

Mrs. Piper opened the front door before they had time to knock. “It’s the birthday girl,” she boomed. She pinched Jamie’s cheek and wrapped her up in a hug. Mr. Piper, as usual, didn’t say much. But he smiled when Jamie told them about feeding Gabe and Donney.

Mr. and Mrs. Piper bundled themselves up and followed the trail back to Jamie’s house.

Mama served hot cocoa while the radio crackled news about the storm. As soon as Daddy was warm, he got ready to go outdoors again. "I'm going to walk to the highway to see if anyone needs help."

Jamie watched from the window as he jumped through the drifts of snow. "Did you see a small dog around here?" she asked Mrs. Piper. "Daddy and I saw tracks when we were checking on Gabe and Donney."

Mrs. Piper pursed her lips. "Someone dumped a puppy in our pasture two days ago," she said. "He wouldn't let us catch him."

Mama put an arm around Jamie's shoulders. "Don't worry," she said. "We'll go looking for the puppy as soon as we can."

Mr. Piper reached in his pocket and pulled out a small flannel bag. "Marbles are a great way to pass a snowy morning. Let's play."

They were sitting on the floor playing a championship game when Daddy returned. Behind him were a young man and a woman with long brown hair. They looked worried and cold. They unwrapped a bundle of blankets as if there was something precious inside.

A tiny baby peeked out at them, then yawned. Jamie liked her powdery smell and sleepy eyes. She leaned over and tickled the baby's soft cheek. "Did you know it's my birthday today?" she whispered.

"I finally got a new job in another town," the young man was saying. "We're moving there now. But our car was stuck in a drift, and it's much too cold for little Sara."

"You're very welcome here," Mama said. She added their snowy coats to the collection in the back hall and heated up the camp stove.

There was a loud knock on the door. “Mercy,” said Mrs. Piper. “Whoever could that be?” The MacDonalds crowded in, mother and father, Laura and Tim.

“Thank heavens we saw the smoke from your chimney,” Mr. MacDonald exclaimed.

“We’d been to visit our grandma for Christmas,” Tim said. “But we got caught in the storm on the way home.”

Mrs. MacDonald was carrying a basket. “A winter picnic,” she said. “Grandma made sandwiches for us to eat in the car. There’s plenty for everyone.”

Mama sliced carrot sticks and crunchy apples to go with the sandwiches. People sat on the floor around the fireplace, eating from paper plates.

"Winter picnics are fun," said Jamie. Everyone agreed.

"No ants or mosquitoes." Mr. MacDonald laughed. He took out a harmonica and played "Baby, It's Cold Outside" while they all sang.

Mrs. Piper rocked Baby Sara and told about blizzards long ago. Laura taught Jamie how to make a cat's cradle out of string. "I know just how you feel," she said. "Last year I had the measles on my birthday. I didn't have a party either!"

Later that afternoon, Daddy and Sara's father went out to see if the snowplow was on the highway. But before very long they returned with a man who was snowy from head to foot.

"I'm the snowplow driver," he said with an embarrassed smile. "My plow went over a hill and got stuck. We'll have to wait until somebody notices I'm missing."

"I think it's time for a birthday party," Mama said. She lit the candles on the cake she'd baked and decorated the night before. There were eleven cheers when Jamie blew out the candles.

Everyone put on party hats and played pin the tail on the donkey. Mrs. Piper was the best. She won a jump rope for her prize.

"What's a party without presents?" said Mr. Piper. He handed Jamie the flannel bag full of marbles. "These belonged to my father. And now they belong to you!"

Sara's mother gave Jamie a comb decorated with tiny seashells. "It's from Florida, where I grew up," she explained. "Now we can both dream of summer beaches on cold winter days."

The MacDonalds gave her the harmonica. “Don’t worry. I’ve got another at home,” said Mr. MacDonald. “We’ll come back in the spring to see how well you play.”

“Quiet,” Mr. Piper said suddenly, and surprised, everyone hushed. From outside came a tiny cry and a scratch on the door.

In came a shaggy puppy, shivering and wet.
"Why, there you are," said Mr. Piper. "I guess you got tired of the cold."
"He must have followed our tracks," Daddy said.
"Maybe he heard how happy we all are inside." Jamie smiled. She and Tim and Laura took turns rubbing the puppy dry with old towels while he wiggled with delight.
Daddy was smiling too. "It looks to me as if another of Jamie's presents has just arrived!"

Mama heated the last of the milk. The birthday puppy licked it up and settled down to sleep on Jamie's lap. Then everyone shouted names.

"Scrappy," said Mrs. MacDonald.

"Poochie," suggested Tim.

But Jamie shook her head. "We'll call him Blizzard. To help us remember this wonderful day."

Outside, the wind had quieted. The sun sparkled like diamond dust over every tree. The television blasted to life with a game show, and everybody jumped, then laughed. From the highway came the sound of snowplows scraping a ribbon of pavement to set the visitors free.

"We hate to go," they said. "We'll write." One by one they hugged and waved and were gone.

9

"Today *was* an adventure," Jamie said later when she kissed her parents good night.

Blizzard looked like a powder puff with a black nose. He licked her hand with his tiny tongue. "This was the best birthday I ever had," Jamie whispered as she tucked him into a basket by her bed. She put the bag of marbles, the harmonica, and the seashell comb on her bedside table. Then she snuggled under the covers, cozy and warm. That night she dreamed of new friends and warm summer days.